Snake
and
Lizard

Joy Cowley / Gavin Bishop

Snake
and
Lizard

GECKO PRESS

Text © Joy Cowley
Illustrations © Gavin Bishop

Reprinted 2007, 2008, 2009

This edition published 2007 by Gecko Press, PO Box 9335,
Marion Square, Wellington 6141, New Zealand
info@geckopress.com

© Gecko Press 2007

National Library of New Zealand Cataloguing-in-Publication Data
Cowley, Joy
Snake and Lizard/by Joy Cowley ; illustrated by Gavin Bishop.
ISBN 978-0-9582787-3-7 (hbk.)—ISBN 978-0-9582720-7-0 (pbk.)
[1. Snakes—Fiction. 2. Lizards—Fiction. 3. Friendship—Fiction.
4. Short stories] I. Bishop, Gavin, 1946-II. Title.
NZ823.2—dc22

ISBN paperback: 978-0-9582787-3-7
ISBN hardback: 978-0-9582720-7-0

Cover & text design: Book Design Limited, Christchurch, New Zealand
Printed by Everbest, China

For more curiously good books, visit www.geckopress.com

To dear Terry who knows that friendship
is not made out of sameness
but the accommodation of differences.

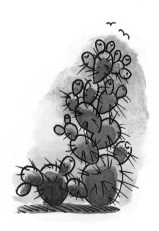

Contents

Heads and Tails

Snake and Lizard came to know each other through an argument, the first of many. This is how it happened.

Snake came out from her hole under the rock, where she had been sleeping all winter. In need of warmth, she looked for a place to sunbathe. The desert round her was stony and spiked with cacti, and Snake wanted a flat smooth patch of earth heated by the sun.

She found the perfect spot and stretched out across it with a comfortable sigh. No sooner had she relaxed than a voice said, 'Excuse me, you're blocking my path.'

Beside her was a lizard who walked and talked in an important way.

'Your path?' murmured Snake.

'Absolutely!' said the lizard. 'Your tail is right across it.'

Snake raised her head. The smooth earth did look like some kind of path but she was too comfortable to move. 'No it isn't.'

'Yes, it is!' cried Lizard. 'It goes from one side of the path to the other.'

'No, it doesn't,' said Snake.

'It does! It does!' said Lizard, jumping up and down. 'I tell you, your tail blocks the entire path.'

'And I tell you it doesn't,' said Snake. 'That's my body, not my tail. The tail is the bit on the end.'

Lizard stopped, his head darting from side to side. 'What body? You don't have a body. Your tail starts at your head.'

'How come you're such an expert on tails?' asked Snake. 'Yours is so short, one hiss and I miss it. You're just envious.'

'Not! Not! Not!' screeched Lizard.

'Yesssssssss!' hissed Snake.

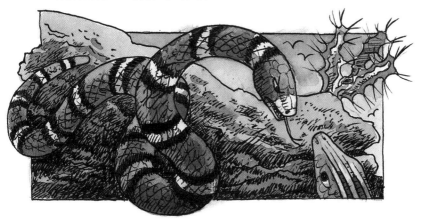

Lizard jumped back and yelled, 'You can never trust a creature without legs!'

'You know your trouble?' Snake shouted back. 'You've got a big mouth.'

The argument could have gone on but now Lizard was getting very upset. He was shaking and blue with rage. Although she was bigger, Snake had only small courage. She knew that when an animal got into

Lizard's state, anything might happen. She drew her body round in a circle so that Lizard could get by.

All the anger went out of him. He sniffed and stood tall. 'Thank you,' he said in a crisp voice.

'Where are you going?' Snake asked.

'To find a place to sunbathe.'

'This is a good spot,' said Snake.

Lizard hesitated.

'Very good,' said Snake, who was feeling that she'd been a bit unfair. 'It's smooth and warm. I'd be happy to share it with you.'

'Really?' said Lizard.

'I'd be glad of the company,' said Snake.

For a while Lizard stood there—his legs leaning in one direction, his head in another. Then he lowered his body to the warm dust.

Above them, the sun shone out of a bright blue bowl of sky. Some early spring bugs were out, flapping or crawling. Lizard opened his mouth and neatly snapped up a green beetle. 'You know,' he said, 'you were an eeny weeny bit right.'

'About what?' asked Snake.

Lizard looked up at the sky. 'Envy,' he said. 'You do have a most remarkable tail.'

Snake smiled. 'And I think your legs are very handsome.'

After that, there was no stopping them. They lay on the path and talked and talked as though they'd known each other for years.

Down By the River

Lizard found Snake on the bank of the river.

'Oh there you are!' said Lizard. 'I've been looking all over for you.'

'Ga-runch!' said Snake.

'Are you all right?' Lizard asked.

'Ga-runch!' Snake said.

Lizard came closer. 'There is something the matter with your voice.'

'Ga-runch! Ga-runch!' said Snake. 'I've got a frog in my throat!' she whispered.

Lizard said, 'Oh, I know how to fix that,' and he gave Snake a mighty slap on her back.

The frog shot out of Snake's mouth. It landed in the grass and, quick as a blink, it hopped away.

'My supper!' cried Snake. 'That was my supper!'

'I'm sorry,' said Lizard. 'I was just trying to help.' Then Lizard smiled. 'Oh Snake, your voice has come back.'

The Picnic

izard and Snake went to the chicken farm for a picnic. Lizard had packed a lunch. 'There's plenty for the two of us,' he said.

Snake looked at the lunch. It was all bugs. There was a dish of moths, a dish of fried flies and some caterpillars.

'Help yourself,' said Lizard, talking with his mouth full.

'No thanks,' said Snake. 'I had a big breakfast.'

Lizard ate quickly. He made loud crunching noises. Snake shivered and shut her eyes.

'What's wrong?' said Lizard.

'If you must know, I think it's disgusting,' said Snake.

'Disgusting?'

'You chew with your mouth open and you've got flies' legs on your chin,' said Snake.

'I am so sorry,' said Lizard in a huffy voice. 'I didn't know I was offending you.'

Snake said, 'I just happen to think that good table manners are important.'

Lizard shut his mouth. He felt angry. He didn't eat any more and he didn't talk.

Now, it was not true that Snake had eaten a big breakfast. She'd had no breakfast at all and her stomach was rumbling. She said, 'Where are the chickens on this farm?'

Lizard sniffed.

'Let's see if we can find some eggs,' said Snake.

Snake went off through the dirt and cacti. Lizard wasn't going to follow, but he didn't want to be on

his own. He ran behind Snake and looked at the sky whenever she talked to him.

Snake found a small hole under the chicken house. As she slithered in, the hens cackled and flew up in a cloud of feathers. Snake slid over to a nesting box. In it were nine fresh eggs. 'Help yourself,' she said to Lizard.

'No thank you,' said Lizard.

Snake opened her jaws and swallowed an egg. She swallowed two more.

'Eating them whole?' cried Lizard. 'Oh that is horrible!'

Snake swallowed three more eggs.

'No biting! No chewing! You can't talk about table manners!'

Another two eggs disappeared.

Lizard went blue with anger. 'I never gulp my food whole. Look at you! I can see the shapes of the eggs inside your skin! Oh! Oh! That really is the most horrible sight!'

Snake gulped the last egg and turned to Lizard with a sleepy smile. 'Please, Lizard, will you widen the hole for me so I can get out again?'

'Why should I?' said Lizard.

'Because you are my friend,' said Snake.

Lizard thought about that. As he scratched dirt away from under the chicken house, he said, 'I've been thinking. Maybe we shouldn't go on picnics together.'

'Thank you,' murmured Snake, and she slid out of the chicken house.

They went back across the farm.

'If we do go on picnics,' said Lizard, 'maybe we should bring our own food.'

'A good idea,' yawned Snake.

'And maybe we should eat with our backs to each other.'

Snake didn't reply. She was fast asleep, curled up under a cactus like a string of striped beads.

Taking Down Walls

Snake lived in a hole under a rock. Lizard moved into the hole next door. The houses were close enough for neighbours but not at all close enough for friends.

'Why don't we live in the same house?' said Lizard.

'Mine,' said Snake quickly.

'No, mine is better,' Lizard said.

'My house has space to curl up in,' Snake said.

'That's fine,' said Lizard, 'but mine is deeper, just right for a creature with legs.'

They argued for a while, and then Snake had an idea. 'Our houses are very close together. If we could scrape away the wall in between, we could have one big house.'

They both agreed that this is what they would do.

Scraping down the wall was hard work. Lizard scratched at the dirt and Snake took it away in her jaws.

Some stones fell down on Snake's tail and she hissed with pain.

'Sorry,' said Lizard.

'That hurts!' said Snake, twitching.

'I told you I was sorry,' Lizard replied. Then he said, 'Look, Snake, when I say that I'm sorry, you should say, "That's okay," and make me feel better.'

'But it's my tail,' said Snake. 'And it isn't okay. It hurts.'

'That doesn't matter,' said Lizard. 'You shouldn't try to make me feel bad just because you feel bad.'

'Did I do that?' Snake said.

'You did.'

'I didn't mean to,' said Snake. 'I know that it was an accident.'

'Exactly,' said Lizard.

'And you did say you were sorry,' Snake said.

'That's good, Snake!' cried Lizard. 'Oh, I can see that you and I are going to get on very well together.'

Snake's tail was feeling better. They went back to work. Lizard stood on his hind legs to scratch away the stones and Snake took them outside in her mouth.

All was going well until Snake tried to pick up a stone which was too big for her. It dropped on Lizard's foot.

'Sorry, Lizard,' she said.

Lizard hopped up and down on three feet. 'Oh, you stupid, slithering hose-pipe! Why can't you be more careful?'

In the Garden

Snake and Lizard were in a garden. Snake was sunbathing in a patch of new corn. Lizard was beside her, catching flies.

A woman came near, to weed the vegetables.

'Uh-uh!' said Snake, with a shudder. 'Here comes that horrible human thing.'

'You shouldn't call anyone names,' said Lizard.

'She is!' said Snake. 'Yesterday she screamed at me.'

'That's because she's scared of you,' said Lizard.

'Scared of me? That's a laugh!'

'It's not funny at all,' replied Lizard. 'You hissed at her. You shouldn't hiss at human things. They don't like it.'

'What should I do?' said Snake.

'Just remember that human things are creatures too, and all creatures need kindness.'

'But human things give me the creeps,' said Snake.

'Don't talk like that,' said Lizard. 'Say to yourself, "I will be kind. I will be kind." Go on!'

Snake curled up amongst the corn, muttering, 'I will be kind. I will be kind,' while Lizard went away to hunt for flies in the lettuce patch.

A little while later, Lizard heard a terrible scream. He saw the gardening woman running into her house, waving her hands.

Lizard went back to Snake, who was shaking with fear.

'Sh-sh-she s-s-screamed at me!'

'You hissed at her!' said Lizard.

'No! No! I was being k-k-kind!'

'What did you do?' said Lizard.

'I just k-k-kissed her!' said Snake.

The Bad Mood

Snake was lying on a warm rock in the sun, when Lizard came along.

'I thought you were hunting for bugs,' said Snake.

'I was,' said Lizard. 'Then I said to myself, "Poor Snake is in a bad mood. I'll go and cheer her up."'

'I'm not in a bad mood,' said Snake.

'You were very quiet this morning,' said Lizard.

'I'm quiet when I'm happy,' said Snake. 'Why shouldn't I be happy? It's a beautiful day.'

'It's all right,' said Lizard. 'You don't have to pretend with me. I'm your friend.'

'Pretend what?'

'That you're in a good mood.'

'But I am in a good mood,' said Snake.

'That's what a friend is for,' said Lizard. 'You can cry on my shoulder. You can tell me all your troubles.'

'I don't have any troubles,' said Snake. 'Please, Lizard, just leave me alone.'

'What?' said Lizard. 'Leave you alone when you need cheering up? Never. I'm going to stay here and make you feel better.'

Snake twitched. 'For the last time, Lizard, I'm not in a bad mood and I don't need cheering up. Why won't you listen?'

Lizard patted Snake on the head. 'Oh Snake, dear! You are always so brave. Well, you don't have to be brave now. Come now, tell Lizard what is wrong.'

'Nothing is wrong!' cried Snake. 'Go away!'

'Not until you feel better,' said Lizard.

Snake raised her head and hissed loudly.

Lizard jumped back in fright. 'What did you do that for?'

'Because I'm in a bad mood,' said Snake.

The Adventure

It was night and Snake was trying to sleep.

'I'm bored,' said Lizard.

'Mmmm,' said Snake.

'Aren't you bored?' Lizard asked.

Snake sighed in the darkness. 'When I'm sleepy, I like being bored.'

'Oh Snake,' said Lizard. 'Don't you ever long for a nice adventure?'

'No,' said Snake, then very carefully, she said, 'What kind of adventure?'

'Some of my cousins are night lizards. They hunt in the dark. Imagine what that would be like. Out there with eyes all about you, gleaming like stars in the shadows.'

Snake shivered from head to tail. 'You're a daytime lizard and I'm a daytime snake. Dark is dangerous. Go to sleep.'

But Lizard wasn't sleepy. 'Let's tell stories. You start.'

'What kind of story?' said Snake.

'A funny story or a scary story. I don't mind. You choose.'

Snake thought for a moment. 'All right, what flaps in the dark and goes OO-OO-OO?'

'I don't know.'

'A ghost.'

There was silence for a while, then Lizard said, 'Is that all?'

'Yes.'

Lizard made a grunting noise. 'That isn't funny or scary. It isn't even a story. Oh Snake, can't you do better than that?'

'I'm sorry,' said Snake. 'It's because I'm sleepy.'

For a while Lizard sat there, flicking his tail back and forth. Then he said, 'I'm going out!'

Snake was suddenly wide awake. 'Where?'

'I don't know,' said Lizard. 'Just out into the night. I've never been in the dark before. I want an adventure.'

Snake was greatly alarmed. 'Please don't! Dear Lizard, there is something you should know. I have night cousins, too, big snakes who—who—'

'Eat lizards?' said Lizard.

'How did you know that?' Snake said.

'Oh Snake!' said Lizard. 'I wasn't born yesterday. Well, I'm off. Are you coming?'

More than anything, Snake wanted to say, no, but she couldn't let Lizard go out on his own. She followed him out of the long tunnel to their front door.

The night was not as dark as she had supposed. There was a moon as big as a giant egg. The rocks and bushes were silver and blossom hung on the cacti like snow, but the shadows were as deep and dark as wells.

'Come on!' Lizard called in an excited voice.

There were scurrying movements everywhere—mice, beetles, geckos, moths. Somewhere, far away, coyotes barked back and forth.

'Be careful!' Snake hissed.

But Lizard was enjoying himself. He snapped up a beetle and ate it. 'Oh Snake, there are bugs here I've never tasted before. This is the place to come for a midnight snack. Look! Another one!'

As Lizard darted out after the beetle, there was a loud HOO-HOO-HOO above them and the beating of wings. A black shadow passed over the silver earth.

Snake hid under a stone as an owl swooped down and grabbed Lizard in its claws.

Lizard squealed and struggled and fell back to the ground. The owl swooped again.

Snake slid out from under the stone and, quick as a blink, was beside Lizard. She raised her head and swayed, hissing angrily at the owl. She must have looked unusually fierce. The owl could have eaten both Snake and Lizard in two gulps, but it didn't. It flapped its wings quickly, braking its flight, and then turned away. For a moment they saw its yellow eyes in the moonlight, and then it was gone over the ocotillo bushes, crying HOO-HOO-HOO!

Without a word, Snake and Lizard turned and made for their burrow. They went so fast down the tunnel that they skidded into the far wall. They were both quivering all over.

Lizard said in a twitchy voice, 'What an adventure!'

'Adventure?' hissed Snake. 'That owl nearly ate us!'

'But we got away,' said Lizard. 'That's what makes it an adventure. Oh Snake, don't hiss like that! Where's your sense of humour?'

Snake shook herself and curled up by the wall. 'If you want to go out again, you can go by yourself,' she said.

'Maybe another time,' said Lizard.

After a while, Snake said, 'Are you still awake?'

'Yes,' said Lizard.

Snake laughed to herself. 'What flaps in the dark and goes OO-OO-OO?'

Lizard jumped. 'That's not funny,' he said.

Surprise

Lizard was bug-hunting near the chicken farm when he found an egg.

It lay in the dust, smooth, white, and round as the moon.

'Oh wondrous luck!' Lizard cried. 'Snake adores chicken eggs. I'll give her a surprise.'

Lizard carefully fitted his jaws round the egg and carried it back across the desert. It was a big egg and heavy. By the time he got to the hole under the rock, he felt that his jaws would never work again. He put the egg on the ground and rolled it down the tunnel. Then he pushed it into the middle of Snake's bed. 'She will be so pleased,' he said to himself. 'I can't wait to see her face.'

He sat at the entrance, watching for Snake. Hours passed. The sun moved from one side of the sky to the other and shadows stretched like fingers over the earth.

'I wish she'd hurry up,' Lizard muttered.

When Snake did appear, just before sunset, Lizard was so relieved that he screamed at her, 'Where have you been?'

'Sorry,' said Snake. 'I fell asleep under a cactus.'

'Don't you know I've been sick with worry?' cried Lizard.

'I said I was sorry.'

Lizard sniffed. 'I've got a surprise for you. I put it on your bed.'

'Oh? What kind of surprise?'

'Go and look,' said Lizard.

Snake slithered down the tunnel. Lizard heard a

strange noise and in the next instant, Snake shot out of the hole, hissing and shaking.

'Y-y-you call yourself m-m-my friend?' she stuttered.

Lizard stared at her. He went down the tunnel and stopped at the entrance to their room. The egg had hatched. No chicken had come out of it! There in Snake's bed, making a noise like a firecracker, was a very angry young rattlesnake.

Lizard moved so fast out of the tunnel that he bumped into Snake. 'I thought it was a chicken egg!'

Snake said, 'What? You mean you don't know the difference between chickens and rattlesnakes?'

'Their eggs look the same.'

'They are not alike in any way!' snapped Snake.

'Well, I'm not an egg fancier,' said Lizard. 'How would I know! I just wanted to surprise you.'

'That wasn't a surprise,' said Snake. 'That was a shock. Tell me, how are you going to get it out of there?'

Lizard didn't say anything.

'It's getting dark,' Snake said.

'I know. I know.'

'We have to go to bed,' she said.

'Don't look at me in that tone of voice!' snapped Lizard. 'You know all about snakes. It's your cousin. Go and talk to it!'

'Some cousins I don't speak to!' cried Snake. 'You put it there. You talk to it.'

They argued angrily, getting nowhere. The sky had turned orange with the setting sun and the cool desert breeze was flapping the yucca bushes like flags. The young rattlesnake showed no sign of coming out. Snake and Lizard had no choice but to crawl into a narrow gap under the rock and settle down for the night.

They were very uncomfortable. The space was hardly big enough for two and they shared it with small stones and dried cactus spines. The cold night wind blew over them with the raw hunting noises of the desert—cries of coyotes, owls, foxes, wildcats. They didn't sleep much. They kept thinking of the warm little room in the earth beneath them.

'I thought I was doing you a favour,' complained Lizard.

'You know what Thought did,' said Snake. 'Thought

thought that his tail was out of bed, so he got out of bed to tuck it in.'

'Sometimes,' said Lizard, 'you can be very sarcastic.'

'Only when someone makes me really mad,' said Snake.

They argued for most of the night—which did help to keep them warm. At some point they must have slept because Lizard opened his eyes to see daylight. The desert was quiet with the soft look of early morning.

He nudged Snake awake. 'Look! Look!'

The little rattlesnake was sliding out of their doorway and down the dusty slope. It moved very slowly, its tongue tasting the air in search of food.

Lizard and Snake stayed until the snake was in the distance, then they rushed towards their door. Side by side, they squeezed down the tunnel and tumbled into their room. They looked round them and sighed with pleasure.

Lizard at once removed the fragments of egg while Snake dusted her bed with her tail, to get rid of the rattlesnake smell.

She and Lizard began to laugh, gently at first, and

then so strongly that they were rolling round the floor with the hiccups.

When they'd stopped, Lizard said, 'Oh Snake! What an adventure!'

Snake's stomach was aching with laughter. 'I don't know why we argue like we do,' she said.

'It's because we're so different,' said Lizard. 'But oh Snake, you are still my best friend.'

'And you are mine, dear Lizard,' said Snake. 'Only do me a favour, please. No more surprises!'

Ancestors

The day was too hot for hunting. Snake and Lizard curled up in a pool of blue shadow under a rock and waited.

'Tell me a story,' said Lizard.

'Okay,' said Snake. 'I'll tell you about my ancestor, the great Sky Serpent.'

'You've told me about her before.'

'This is different,' said Snake. 'It's the story about the dragon's eggs.'

'Dragons are my ancestors,' cried Lizard, flicking and twitching with excitement.

Snake began, 'On the other side of the stars lives a dragon made of fire. Every morning it lays a fiery egg on the edge of the earth. The egg travels across the sky. It will hatch into another fiery dragon and burn up the whole world. But my ancestor, the great Sky Serpent, comes to the rescue. She eats the dragon's eggs.'

'She does not!' cried Lizard.

'The egg is what we call the sun,' explained Snake. 'Just before evening, it slides down into the great Sky Serpent's mouth.'

Lizard twitched all over. 'That's a lie!'

'The next day the fire dragon lays another egg, and the same thing happens,' said Snake.

Lizard cried, 'You think I'm some kind of stupid to believe that garbage?'

'It's only a story, Lizard,' Snake said.

'Well, I don't like it!' snapped Lizard. 'You and your ancestors! Huh! I'll tell you a better story. This big Fire Dragon, my ancestor, gobbled up the Sky Serpent who was eating her eggs.'

'No, she didn't,' said Snake. 'You're making it up.'

'It's my story,' said Lizard.

'But it isn't the right story,' said Snake. 'The dragon didn't eat the serpent.'

'Yes, she did!'

'No, she didn't!'

'Did, did, did!'

'Didn't! Didn't! Didn't!'

'She ate up all the serpents in the world!' shouted Lizard.

'You've got a nasty tongue!' said Snake. She slid away until she was some distance from Lizard, and tucked her head into the coils of her body. She was feeling deeply hurt.

Lizard yelled at her, 'My ancestors were so dragons! It's true!'

Snake didn't answer. She didn't even raise her head.

'I wish I was a dragon,' said Lizard. 'Then I'd show you!'

Snake lay still. She knew that there was one thing Lizard couldn't stand, and that was silence.

Lizard was muttering, 'If someone came along and

gave me a wish, that's what I'd be. A great fiery dragon. Well, two wishes.' He raised his voice again. 'I said, I'd ask for two wishes so you can have a wish too, Snake. We'd have to be fair.'

Snake wriggled slightly but didn't reply.

'What would you wish?' asked Lizard.

Snake was silent.

Lizard repeated in a coaxing voice, 'Snake, what would you want to be?'

'A centipede,' said Snake at last.

'Centipede?'

'Yes.'

'Not a great Sky Serpent?'

'No.'

Lizard said, 'Why a centipede?'

'Legs,' said Snake.

Lizard crawled over to Snake. 'If I were a fiery dragon and you were a centipede, I don't suppose we could be friends.'

'Right,' said Snake.

Lizard rested his head on Snake's back. 'Maybe we should stay as we are,' he said.

Secrets

The midday sun roasted the desert, and all creatures disappeared into any shade they could find.

Snake and Lizard were under the shelf of a rock. Lizard's stomach was full of large blue flies and he wanted to sleep, but Snake was in a talking mood.

'Tell me, dear Lizard, what was the worst thing you ever did?'

He ignored her.

'I mean, you know, the really worst, most horrible thing in your whole life?'

'Ah—ah—I don't know,' Lizard said.

But Snake would not be put off. 'Come on.'

Lizard turned away. 'I forget.'

'Then remember!' said Snake.

'I don't want to remember.'

'Now, Lizard, look at me! Aren't I the best friend you ever had? Can't you trust me to the end of time? Okay? So get it off your chest!'

Lizard gave a long shivering sigh. 'It happened a long time ago. I lost my little brother.'

'That's it?'

'Yeah.'

'That's the worst?'

'I never found him again,' Lizard said.

Snake was disappointed. 'You told me you had ninety-seven brothers and sisters. No offence, but what's so terrible about losing one?'

'He was the youngest,' Lizard replied. 'A real sweet little guy. I was supposed to take him fly fishing down by the drain, but he was so slow I left him behind. When I came back he was g-g-gone.' Lizard's full belly shook with sobs.

'Take it easy, dear buddy!' Snake rested her head near his. 'Maybe he just waddled off into the desert and got adopted by another lizard family.'

'No. He wouldn't have done that.'

'Well, maybe he went home without you. I mean, did you count?'

'He didn't go home.'

'Are you sure?'

'Sure, I'm sure. I told him to stay put, and my little brother was very obedient.'

'I know what happened,' said Snake. 'You came back to the wrong place.'

Lizard shook his head. 'I left him in the hollow of an old dead cactus shaped like a coyote's head.'

'You did?'

'I was only gone two minutes,' sobbed Lizard.

Snake moved away and said, 'There must be hundreds of old dead cactuses shaped like coyote's heads.'

'Nope. Only one.'

At that, Snake became quiet from her head to the tip of her tail. She was remembering a time when she had been slithering through the desert, looking for lunch. There, in front of her, had been a big old cactus with dead branches sticking up like a coyote's ears.

In a split near the bottom was a fat little lizard. The silly thing didn't move, and Snake had not been able to stop herself. Lizard was right. The little guy had been real sweet.

After a long, shuddering sob, Lizard got his breath back and said to Snake, 'Your turn.'

'My turn what?'

'You know. Your turn to say the very worst thing you ever did.'

'Oh, that,' said Snake. She thought for a moment. 'I hissed at my mother,' she said.

Money

Snake was sliding through the desert when she found a ten cent coin. She picked it up in her mouth and took it back to Lizard. 'What's this?'

Lizard became very excited. 'Money! Oh Snake, what a find!'

'It doesn't taste very good,' said Snake.

Lizard turned the coin over. 'Human things collect these. They use them to go into business.'

'What's business?' asked Snake.

Lizard looked vague. 'You wouldn't understand, Snake. It's all to do with buying and selling.'

'Trading?'

'Well—yes. Kind of,' said Lizard.

'Then why don't we go into business?' said Snake.

Lizard thought about that. 'It's not easy. The main thing about business is we have to sell something which everyone wants to buy.'

'Like food and drink?' asked Snake.

Lizard stared at her, with his mouth open. 'Oh Snake! There are times when you're very clever!'

'My ancestors were known for their wisdom,' Snake murmured.

'Food and drink it is,' said Lizard. 'You can sell cactus juice and I'll sell corn cakes. Tomorrow we'll open two stalls.'

'Who'll buy from us?' asked Snake.

'All the desert creatures.'

'Yes, but where will they get money?'

'The same way you did,' said Lizard. 'They'll find it.'

Snake thought there was something wrong with that but she didn't argue. Lizard knew best about these things.

For the rest of the afternoon Snake gathered cactus fruit and crushed them in her jaws. She collected the juice in a clay pot.

Lizard went to the village to get some corn from a human thing's garden. He spent the rest of the day making corn cakes.

They were both so excited about their new business that they hardly slept that night. At the first pinkness of dawn, they went out to set up their stalls. Lizard painted signs on the rocks: CACTUS JUICE 10 CENTS A CUP was in front of Snake's clay pot and CORN CAKES 10 CENTS EACH was by his own. They waited for their first customers.

A number of small creatures went by but none of them stopped. The sun came up, high and hot, and Lizard was feeling thirsty.

He picked up the ten cent coin which Snake had found. 'Oh Snake, could I please buy a cup of your delicious cactus juice?'

'Of course, Lizard,' said Snake. She poured him a cup and took the coin. 'My first sale,' she cried.

But now Snake was hungry, and Lizard's corn cakes smelled very good. She held out the coin. 'May I buy a corn cake, please?'

'You certainly may,' said Lizard. 'And when you've finished eating it, I'll have another large cup of that wonderful cactus juice.'

This went on for the rest of the morning. Snake bought all of Lizard's corn cakes and Lizard bought all of Snake's cactus juice. By the middle of the day there was nothing left.

Snake looked at their empty stalls. 'I really don't understand business,' she said. 'I sold all my cactus juice at ten cents a cup. You sold all your corn cakes at ten cents each. And we still have only ten cents.'

Lizard thought about it. 'We did it right,' he said. 'It should have worked out.'

'Never mind,' said Snake. 'It's been a fun morning.'

Lizard smiled. 'Yes, it has. Let's go into business again some time.'

Then Lizard picked up their clay pots and together they went back home, leaving the ten cent coin shining in the desert sand.

Helpers

Snake and Lizard were travelling through the desert in very serious conversation.

'What do you want to do with your life?' Lizard said to Snake.

'I want to be a helper,' said Snake. 'I really like helping.'

'So do I,' said Lizard. 'I think I'll be a helper too. Both of us! Isn't that something?'

Snake smiled at Lizard. 'You're my dearest friend, Lizard. You have first call on my time. When you need help, just let me know.'

'That's nice of you, Snake,' said Lizard. 'But you forget that I'm a helper too. Helpers give help. They don't take it.'

'That's right!' said Snake. 'I forgot.'

Snake and Lizard went further into the desert, talking, wondering how they could set up a helping business. After a long time, Lizard stopped and looked around them. 'Do you know where we're going?'

Snake raised her head to study the stones and bushes. 'No.'

'I think we've come too far,' said Lizard.

At that moment a jack rabbit hopped out from behind a cactus. 'Hey! You two look lost. Do you need some help?'

'No thank you,' said Lizard. 'We are helpers.'

'Helpers give help,' explained Snake. 'They don't take it.'

'Okay,' shrugged the rabbit, and it hopped away to nibble on a bush.

Lizard and Snake were looking at the rabbit and they didn't notice that they were on the bank of the river. The sand under them crumbled and the next instant they were rolling down the bank and into the water. At once, the current swept them away.

They were lucky that there were some rocks near the edge of the river.

They were washed against the rocks and were able to pull each other out of the water. They were very cold. They lay in the sun, shivering and gasping.

'Did you see that rabbit?' said Snake. 'He just sat and looked at us.'

'Rabbits are like that,' said Lizard.

Snake coughed out another bit of river. Then she said, 'I've been thinking about Snake and Lizard, Helper and Helper.'

'Lizard and Snake,' said Lizard.

'I've been thinking that maybe we should be allowed to take help as well as give it.'

Lizard was silent for a long time. Then he said, 'All right, but only when we need it.'

Help!

izard put out a sign: LIZARD AND SNAKE—HELP AND HELPER, but three days passed and no one came for help. Then, on the fourth day, while Snake was asleep, a small creature scratched by the entrance to their house.

Lizard went up the tunnel calling, 'Coming! Coming!'

Snake dreamily listened to Lizard's voice answering

a shrill nervous squeak. When she realised what was happening she raised her head. Someone out there needed help! Their first client.

She slid up the tunnel, put her head out the hole and saw Lizard talking to a small round mouse.

The mouse was in such a state! It jittered about, squeaking and wiping its front paws together. Lizard was making soft slow noises which sounded like comfort and good advice.

Snake didn't hear what was being said. She was too busy staring at the mouse which was as plump as any she had ever seen. It was all roundness. She felt a shiver start at her tail and go up her body to her mouth. Before she could stop herself her jaw dropped open to the size of the mouse. She closed it quickly but the thought was still there. What a sweet little mouse! How plump! How perfect!

She couldn't bear to watch it. She slipped backwards into the house and tried to go back to sleep. But the thoughts kept running round in her head and she could actually feel the mouse in her mouth. Mouse, mouth, mouse, mouth, she said to herself until the two

words became one. Then a new thought, bolder and more wicked, came to her. Why didn't she go up there and assist Lizard? She could take the little mouse for a short walk in the desert. Very short.

She slithered quickly outside and blinked in the bright light. Lizard was on his own.

'Where's the mouse?'

'I sent it to stay with relations,' said Lizard, returning to the tunnel. As he came in, Snake slid back and swallowed her disappointment. 'It'll be safe there,' Lizard said.

'What was the problem?' Snake asked.

'Poor little creature,' said Lizard. 'A big snake wanted to eat it. Can you imagine such a thing?'

Snake didn't answer. She tucked her head in a corner and pretended she was asleep.

Self-help

Snake and Lizard were in business. Along with the Help and Helper sign, they now had two other signs outside their door.

One said: EXPERT HELP GIVEN, NO PROBLEM TOO BIG OR TOO SMALL. The second new sign was Snake's idea. It said: PAYMENT: ONE FLY OR BEETLE FOR SMALL HELP, ONE QUAIL'S EGG FOR BIG HELP.

Lizard had not been too sure about these charges. 'I like flies and beetles,' he said. 'You like quails' eggs.'

'So?'

'So I get the little jobs and you get the big ones.'

'No, no!' Snake replied. 'Lizard dear, it doesn't work that way. All it means is I give you the flies and beetles I get and you give me your quails' eggs.'

'Oh,' said Lizard. 'I see.'

The first visitor was a rabbit, who jumped around as though the earth were red hot.

'Hey, you guys! I need some help, aid, assistance, a friendly paw.'

Snake smiled. 'Paw, no. Help, yes. What can we do for you?'

'It's a tortoise,' the rabbit said. 'He came down my burrow when I was out, and he won't leave. I need you to get rid of him.'

'Rid of him?' said Snake.

'Yeah. You know—move, throw, toss, expel, kick him out.'

'I'm sorry, sir,' said Snake. 'That's not the sort of helping we do. We are counsellors.'

'What's that?' asked the rabbit, hopping from one side to another.

'We don't *do* things. We *say* things. We help you to help yourself.'

'Oh,' said the rabbit. 'You mean like advice, wisdom, handy hints?'

'Exactly,' said Snake. She slid closer to the rabbit. 'Now, this tortoise, this new friend in your burrow—'

The rabbit jumped back. 'He's no friend of mine! Enemy, villain, intruder, pain in the neck!'

'But couldn't you possibly become friends?' Snake asked.

The rabbit's face shone red under his fur. 'No! You're supposed to be helping me!' he screeched.

Lizard rushed over. 'Excuse me! Excuse me, sir! Have you tried asking this tortoise to leave?'

'Leave as in go, depart, scram? Sure I have! He just pulls his head into his shell. You ever try pushing a stubborn tortoise out of a burrow? It's all uphill!'

'Then there's only one thing to do,' said Lizard. 'Tell him you're renting the burrow to a large rattlesnake.'

'What?' The rabbit jumped again. 'Are you crazy, loopy, bonkers?'

Lizard said, 'But you're not really renting to a rattlesnake.'

'No?'

'Just pretending.'

The rabbit grinned. 'You mean I tell a lie, fib, whopper?'

'Well—er—yes,' said Lizard.

'Hey! That might just work!' The rabbit laughed. 'Thanks, pal. You've been a big help.'

'Big help costs one quail's egg,' said Lizard.

For the rest of the morning a stream of creatures came to Snake and Lizard.

Some had big problems, some had small problems.

75

Lizard and Snake listened, gave good advice, and collected payment. Behind them a pile of flies, beetles and quails' eggs steadily grew.

Early in the afternoon, a snappy tortoise arrived. He stomped his flat feet in the dust and growled. 'Do something!'

'Pardon me?' said Snake.

'You're helpers, aren't you? Do something about that pesky rabbit in my burrow. He's renting to a rattlesnake!'

'Let us have a few details, sir,' said Snake. 'Now, whose burrow did you say?'

'Mine!' snapped the tortoise. 'It was empty when I found it.'

'Ah, but who *made* the burrow?' Lizard asked.

'What do I care who made the burrow? The whole point is he's bringing in a giant rattler. He's crazy!'

'Bad news, bad news,' sighed Lizard.

'Rattlesnakes have mean tempers. They also bite other reptiles—of the hard shell variety.'

Snake nodded. 'Our advice to you, sir, is for you to find another home.'

'Far away,' said Lizard. 'Far away.'

The tortoise rumbled with anger. 'You're not much help!' she snapped.

'Little help costs one beetle,' said Snake.

As the tortoise stomped off, Lizard ran around the heap of flies and beetles. 'Are you hungry, Snake?' he asked.

'Starving!' Snake replied, her tongue flickering with pleasure.

But at that moment a group of quails ran up the path, their feathers all in a fuss. Snake quickly draped herself over the eggs and pretended she was asleep.

'We need help!' one of the quails squawked at Lizard. 'Everyone keeps robbing our nests!'

'I'm sorry,' said Lizard. 'I'm really very sorry. But we're closed for the day.'

The River of Death

Early one morning, Snake and Lizard heard a snuffling noise at their door. Snake was going to call, 'Who's there?' but as soon as she opened her mouth, she knew. 'Good morning, Skunk.'

She and Lizard went out to talk to the skunk who stood by their door, slowly waving his tail. 'I heard you two were in the helping business.'

'That's right,' said Lizard. 'You need help?'

Skunk sighed, 'Fact one, I'm in love.'

'That's nice,' said Snake.

'Fact two, she's the most wonderful skunk I've ever seen.'

'Then go to her!' cried Lizard.

'Fact three, she lives on the other side of the river of death.'

'Oh!' said Lizard and Snake together. Then Lizard said, 'Well, you know, the world is full of lovely lady skunks.'

'I must be with her!' Skunk said.

Snake hissed with fear. 'No one crosses the river of death!'

'I can if you two help me,' Skunk replied.

Snake and Lizard jumped. 'That's not the kind of helping we do,' Lizard said.

Skunk gave them a sad smile. 'I don't want you to go across the river with me. That would be dangerous for you. No, no. I want you to take me to the edge. Give me courage. Say comforting words.'

Snake and Lizard thought about this, then Lizard said, 'All right, Skunk. We'll help. But only to the edge.'

So Snake and Lizard set out on each side of Skunk, towards the river of death. The desert was still cool with morning shadows and birds everywhere were calling up the sun.

Snake said, 'Skunk, do you know how many monsters there are on that river?'

Skunk said, 'Fact one, thousands of animals are killed each year. Fact two, the river of death has no end. Fact three, I can't live without her.'

'You might die without her,' said Lizard. 'That's not much of a choice.'

Snake paused. 'Listen! The monsters!'

They stopped, their hearts beating faster. Ahead of them lay the grey river, harder than desert sand and filled with raging monsters which never slept. By night their eyes shone brighter than the moon. During the day, the sun glittered on their hard, hairless skins. They moved so fast that no one could escape them.

Sometimes, they made loud honking noises. Always, they roared.

'Say something to cheer me!' Skunk said in a faint voice.

'I've got a cheerful story,' Lizard replied. 'One day my mother was sitting in a mesquite tree near the river of death, when two monsters attacked each other, head to head. What a noise! What anger! Bits of them were scattered over the river, as far as the mesquite tree. My mother picked up a piece that looked like sharp ice, only it didn't melt. Of course, the monsters killed each other. Other monsters came and dragged them away. He looked at Skunk. 'Does that make you feel better?'

'No,' said Skunk, shivering.

Snake leaned against him and said, 'Think about your love.'

Skunk blinked at her, then smiled. 'Her eyes are like dark caves,' he said. 'Her coat is a midnight sky striped with moonlight. Her perfume is—'

But they didn't hear what her perfume was, for they were near the river of death and the monsters were

rushing past with a noise like thunder. As each swept by, a wave of wind blew Snake and Lizard backwards and ruffled Skunk's fur.

'Please, don't go!' Snake said.

'Love is stronger than death,' Skunk said. 'Goodbye, my friends. Thank you for helping me.'

'There's a gap coming,' said Lizard. 'Wait. Right! Go now!'

Almost as soon as Skunk had ambled out onto the river of death, another crowd of monsters raced by in a fury. Snake and Lizard shut their eyes. 'Think about love,' Snake said to Lizard. 'Think about love.'

The roar of the monsters passed and Snake and Lizard dared to look. Neither of them could see very well but they could make out something black, lying out there, flat and still.

'Stupid skunk!' cried Lizard.

Snake sniffed and tasted the air. 'No!' she said. 'It is definitely not Skunk. It must be the black stuff the monsters wear on their feet.' She sniffed again and smiled. 'He got across! Lizard, he got to the other side!'

'Well,' said Lizard, 'I always thought that he would. After all, he had us to help him. Oh Snake, I'm hungry. Let's go home and find some breakfast.'